CHASED by a BEAR

By Virginia McCaffrey • Illustrated by Robin Boyer

"Good Night, Grandad!"
"See you in the morning!"
"Love you!"

The four grandchildren were off to bed and couldn't wait to get there.
It was Saturday night and that meant another one of their weekly sleepovers
with their grandparents.

"What's the hurry? I've never seen children so excited to go to bed before," wondered Grandad.

"You'd need to see it to believe it. I'm going to tuck them in and tell them a story, " Nany said, as she kissed his cheek.

Brian, William, Allyson, and Virginia ran to the bedroom that Nany designed just for them and leaped across the room onto the bed. They couldn't wait for Nany's story and the *adventure* to begin...

Once the children were tucked into bed, ready for the night's story, they grabbed each other's hands like they had dozens of times before. You see, Nany's stories weren't normal bedtime stories like other grandmothers would tell. They learned a long time ago that if they were holding hands when Nany said "*Story Time*", in a singing tone, they were magically whisked away and became a part of an adventure. No one but the five of them knew just why story time was so special with Nany, not even Grandad.

With their hands clenched tightly together, the adventure began.

"Story Time..."

It was late at night and the moon was full. The only thing they could hear was the howling of a coyote in the distance, but it was enough to frighten the four children. Nany knew it could get dangerous at night in the woods and that they needed to find shelter.

They started their hike through the woods.
Allyson was the first one to spot the cabin. It was down the hill, between
the two biggest pine trees the children had ever seen.

The five of them headed to the cabin, when they heard the snarling growl of a ferocious bear just behind them! They picked up the pace and ran as fast as their legs could carry them!

Luckily, the cabin was unlocked and they all dove right through the entrance and slammed the door before the bear could follow.

They needed a plan. How could they leave the cabin and get back to Nany's house if they were trapped by a BEAR? They needed to get back to where the story began and all say, *'THE END!'* in order to return to the bedroom where they'd be tucked in and ready for sleep.

William and Brian came up with a great idea. If they could find a way to distract the bear and lead him away from the cabin, they could run back up the hill to where their story started.

"Hey guys! Do you think these could work?" Virginia and Allyson found a bedroom with a chest that was filled to the top with firecrackers.

"That's perfect, girls! We can light the firecrackers and *scare* the *bear*! Maybe he won't like the loud sounds and run away," said Nany.

There was just one problem. How were they going to light the firecrackers? There was no fire in the fireplace and no one had matches. They were all in their *pajamas*!

Nany led the children into the kitchen. She searched the cabinets hanging high on the walls while the children searched the ones below.

"Ah-ha! Perfect!" Brian found a book of matches in the cabinet with the pots and pans. But there was *ANOTHER* problem!

"There's only one match in here." said William. "We can't mess this up! We only have *ONE* chance to light the firecrackers and *scare* the *bear* away!"

The children all agreed that it would be safer to have Nany light the match. She went to the back door of the cabin and tiptoed her way to the front porch, being careful not to let the bear see her.

14

Inside the cabin, Brian, William, Allyson, and Virginia were standing at the front door, ready to bolt out the door and up the hill.

Nany told the children "Once it is lit, we've got to move quickly. 1...2...3..." and in the blink of an eye the match was lit and she was holding it to the firecracker fuse.

16

Within seconds it sounded as if a *HUGE* explosion were occurring, with sparks that lit up the sky!

Nany waved to the front door, "Let's GO! Run as fast as you can"
and the children were on their way, sprinting up the big hill.
As they were running, Nany looked over her shoulder.
The bear had spotted them and was coming right for them.
 "Kids! Keep going. He is right behind us!"
They had never run so fast in their entire lives!

With their little legs pumping as fast as they could, they reached the top of the hill. They once again held hands and quickly said in unison,

"THE END!"

Before they knew it, they were back in the bedroom, huddled on the bed and laughing.
 "Wow! THAT was a close one!" said Will.
 "I know! I wasn't sure how we were going to get out of there this time," replied Allyson through her laughter.

"What's going on down here? I thought these kids were going to bed."
It was Grandad standing in the doorway to the bedroom. He had *NO IDEA*
that while he was snacking on pepperoni and pretzels and watching television,
the five of them had been on an *adventure*.

"Ok, ok they were just settling down to go to sleep," Nany said with a wink
to the children.

Nany and Grandad kissed each of the children on the head, turned out the light, and headed down the hall.

"You need to be stricter with them at bedtime. What caused all the excitement?" the children could hear Grandad ask Nany from outside the room.

"You'd need to see it to believe it," said Nany.

The four children lay wide awake, trying to catch their breath before they fell asleep. Brian whispered to Allyson, Will and Virginia, "I wonder where Nany's story will take us *next week...*"

For Nany.
Your unconditional love and support was one of a kind. Your Army Club meetings, shopping dates at the "Everything Store" and "Meeting Time" will live on in our memories.
-VM

For my Gran and all of your love and support in my artistic ways as I took over the kitchen table with buckets of crayons, stacks of paper, glue, and tape to create summer visit masterpieces.
-RB

Made in the USA
Lexington, KY
26 September 2017